The Glass Mountain

RETOLD BY DIANE WOLKSTEIN

ILLUSTRATED BY LOUISA BAUER

Morrow Junior Books · New York

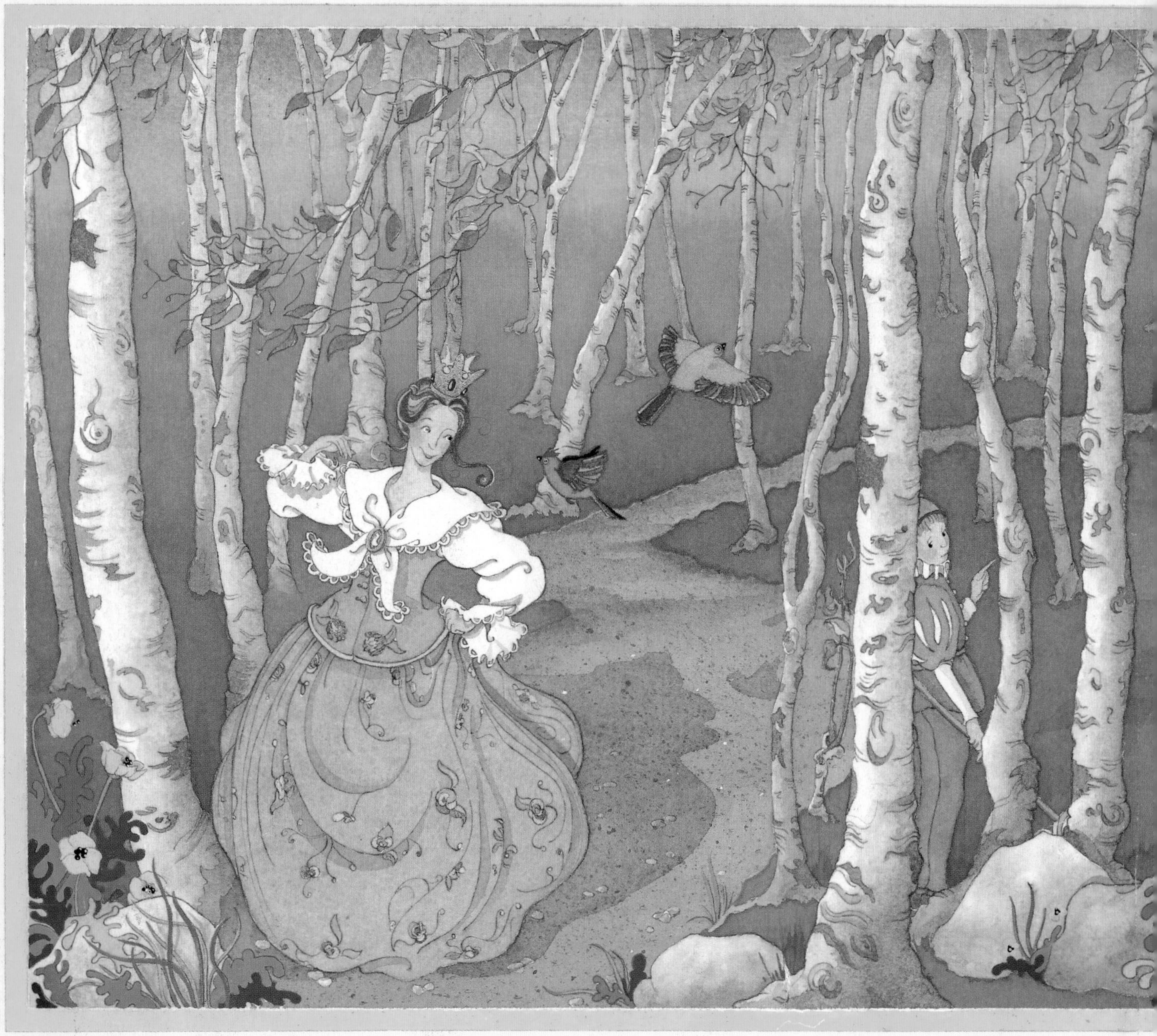

GOLD, CRIMSON, ROSE, YELLOW, PURPLE, ORANGE, LIME GREEN—these were the colors the princess loved. She also loved to wander in the woods, listening to the songs of the birds. Her servants followed at a distance, and

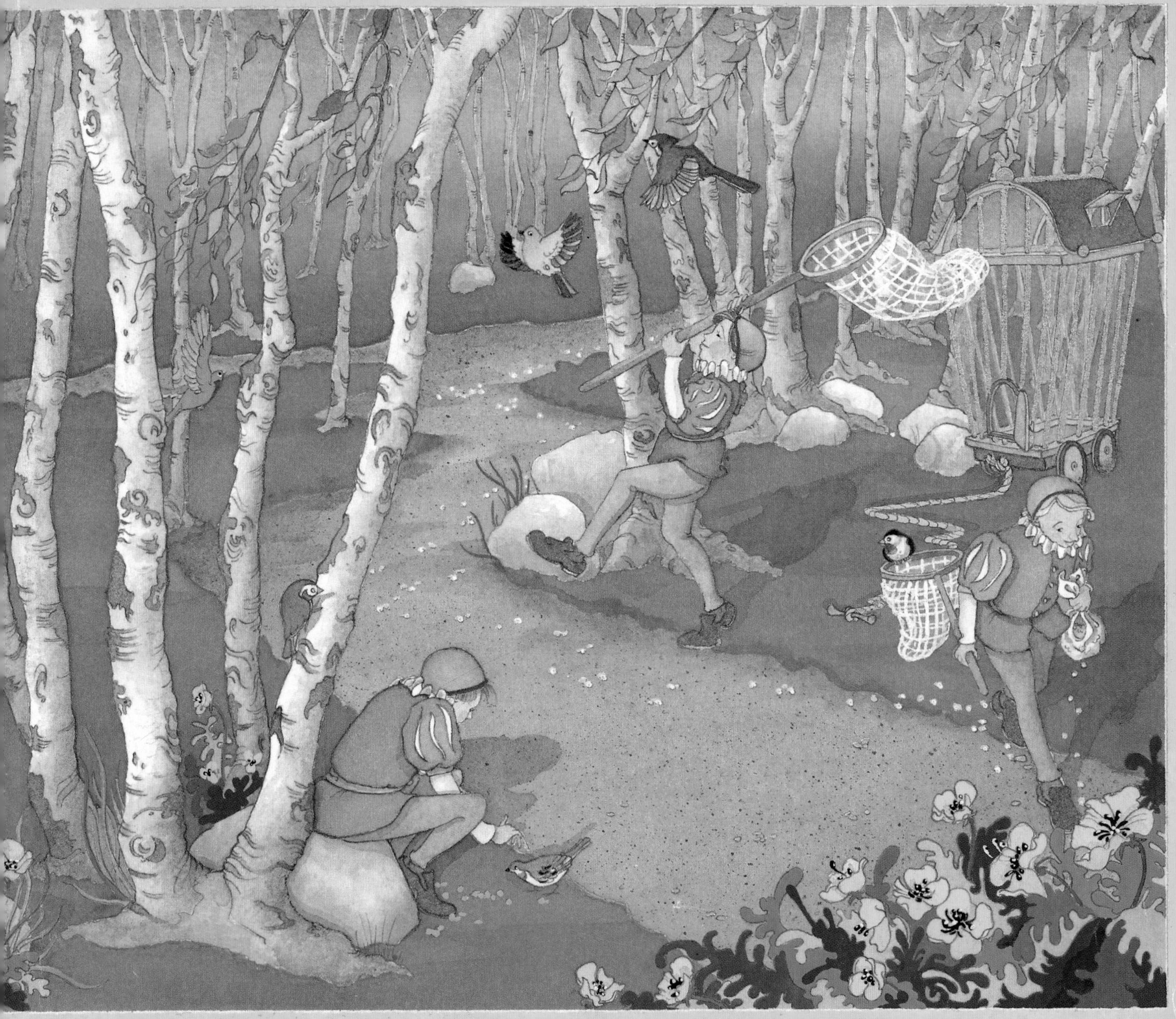

to please her, they caught the birds whose songs she enjoyed and brought them back to the palace to put in cages. Her father, the king, had named her Raina, for when she smiled, she was as radiant as the sun.

When it came time for Raina to marry, her father worried. Raina's mother had died in childbirth, and the king had become both mother and father to his daughter. He wanted to find a young man who would cherish and love Raina as much as he did.

At the edge of town there was a wood, and beyond the wood, a stream, and on the other side of the stream there was a barren place where no trees grew. The king decided to have a glass mountain built on the barren place, and then he sent notices throughout the kingdom announcing: *The first man who can climb the glass mountain may marry the princess and become the next king.*

Many men arrived at the palace eager to be king. Each afternoon a suitor entered the throne room and bowed to the princess. And the next morning, no matter what the weather, he had to climb the mountain. Many men tried, but the glass mountain was steep and very slippery, and each of the suitors slipped and fell—and many died.

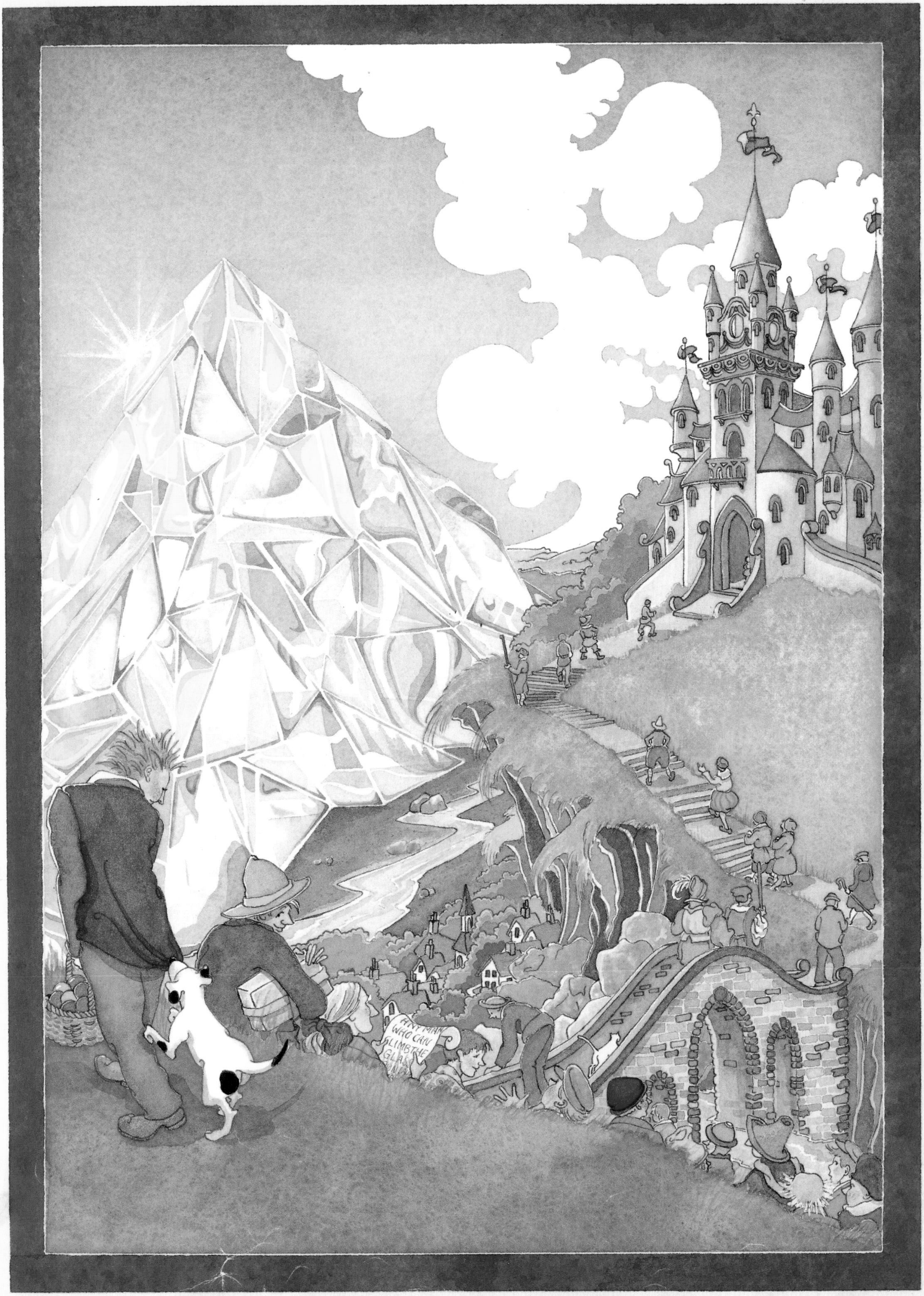
ANY MAN
WHO CAN
CLIMB THE

Then there came a young man named Jared. After Jared bowed to the princess, he brought his crimson hat to his heart and blushed. The princess smiled, and Jared exclaimed, "A ray of sunshine!" and burst into such merry whistling that all the caged birds in the palace began to sing. "I hear a lark in the palace!" he said. "And a warbler as well!" He then whistled the song of the lark. Again the birds sang. And Raina said, "Please stay so I too can learn to whistle the song of the lark."

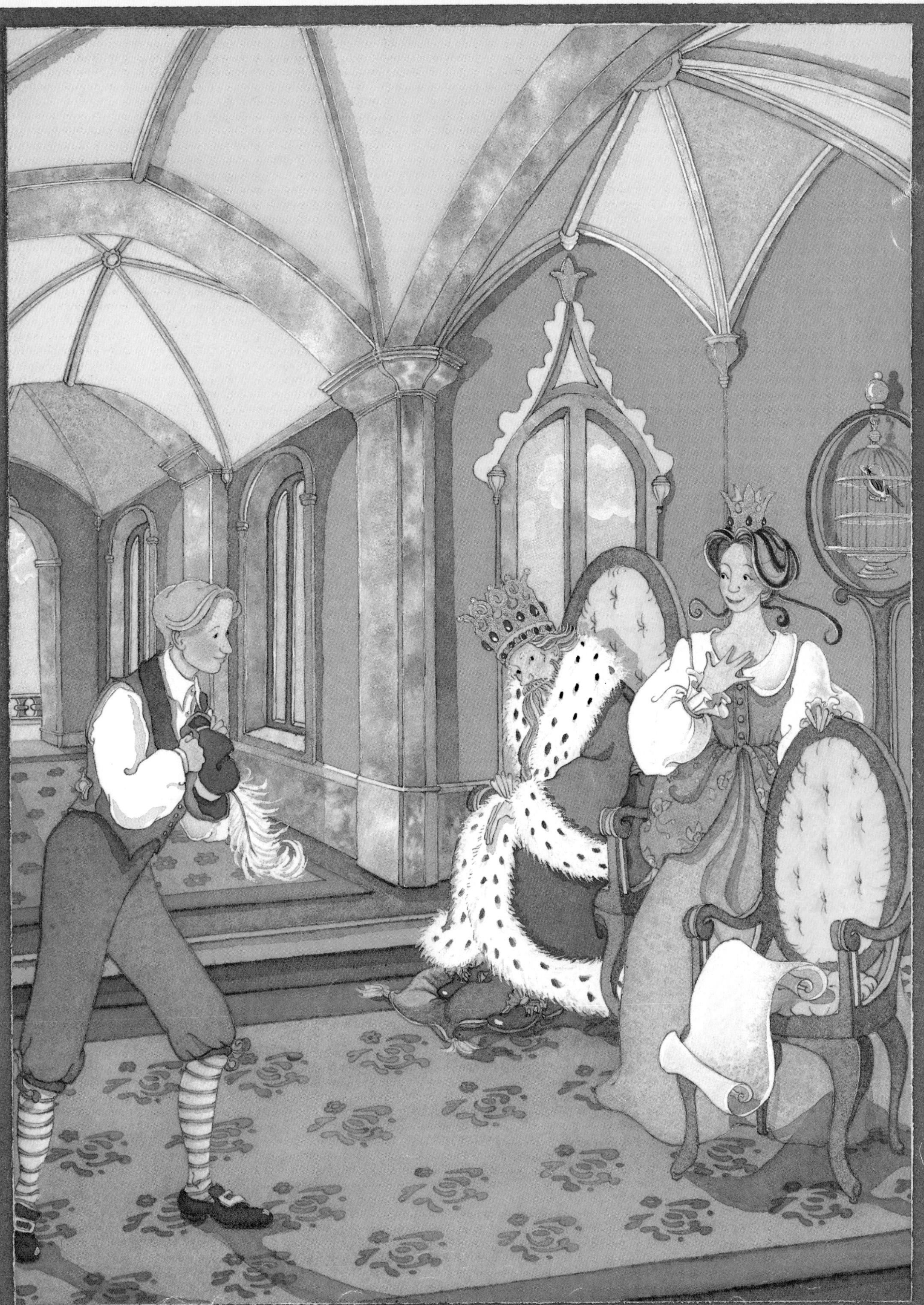

The next morning the princess was waiting at the foot of the glass mountain. She was wearing a rose-colored cap, a yellow dress, purple leggings, and no shoes. She said to Jared: "I will go with you and help you. The mountain is slippery, so I have taken off my shoes." Barefoot and holding hands, they started up the mountain. The people in the town watched them go higher and higher.

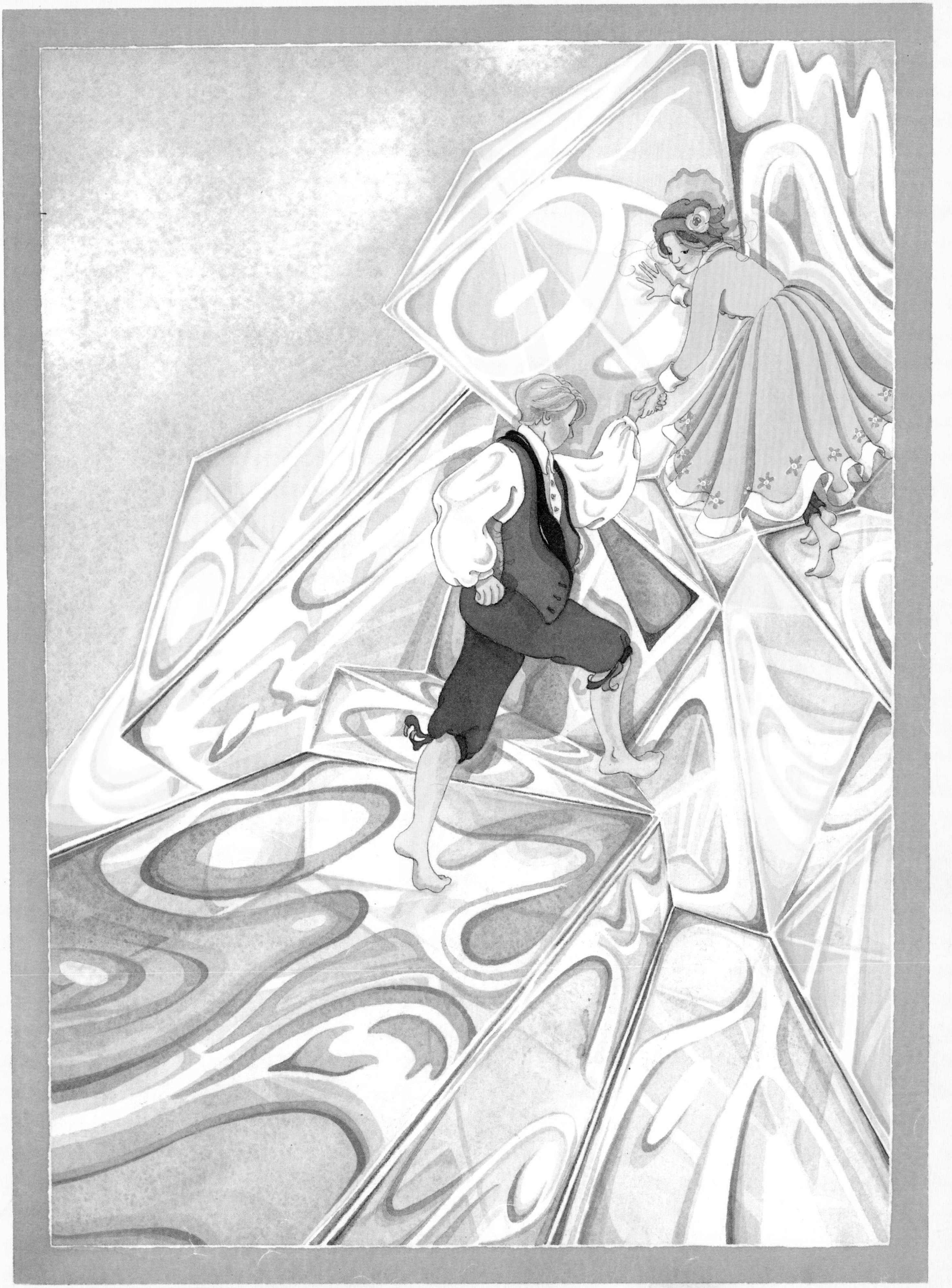

They were nearly at the top when Raina stepped on a crack, lost her balance, and let go of Jared's hand. "Rai-na! *Rai-naa!*" Jared cried as he rolled down the mountain.

He scrambled to his feet and tried to climb back up, but he could not climb the mountain without her. In despair, he went back to the king. The king and Jared returned to the mountain, but Raina had disappeared.

Raina had fallen through a crack,
down,
down,
down,
down,
through the glass mountain, and
down,
down,
down,
under the earth into a cave.

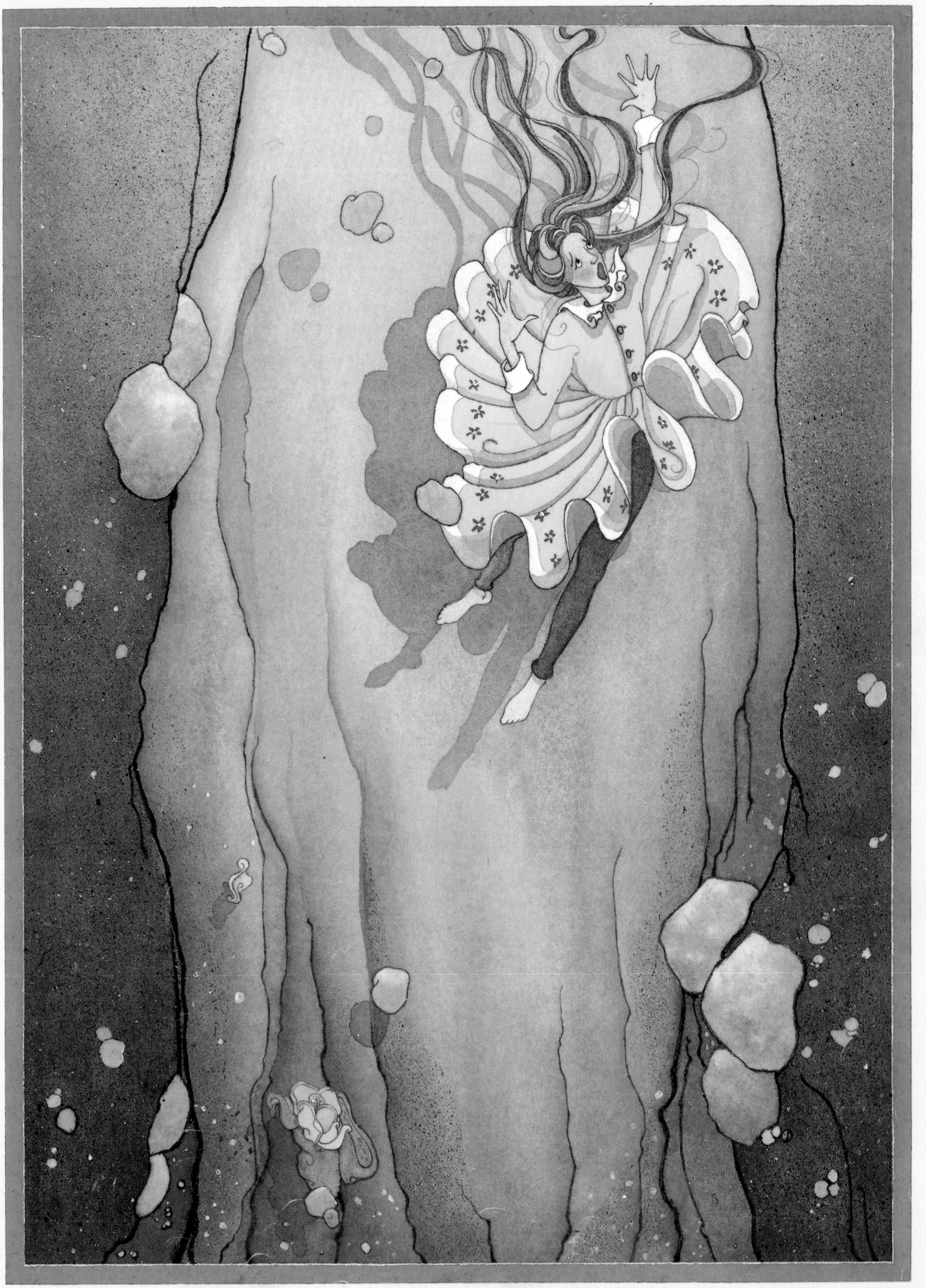

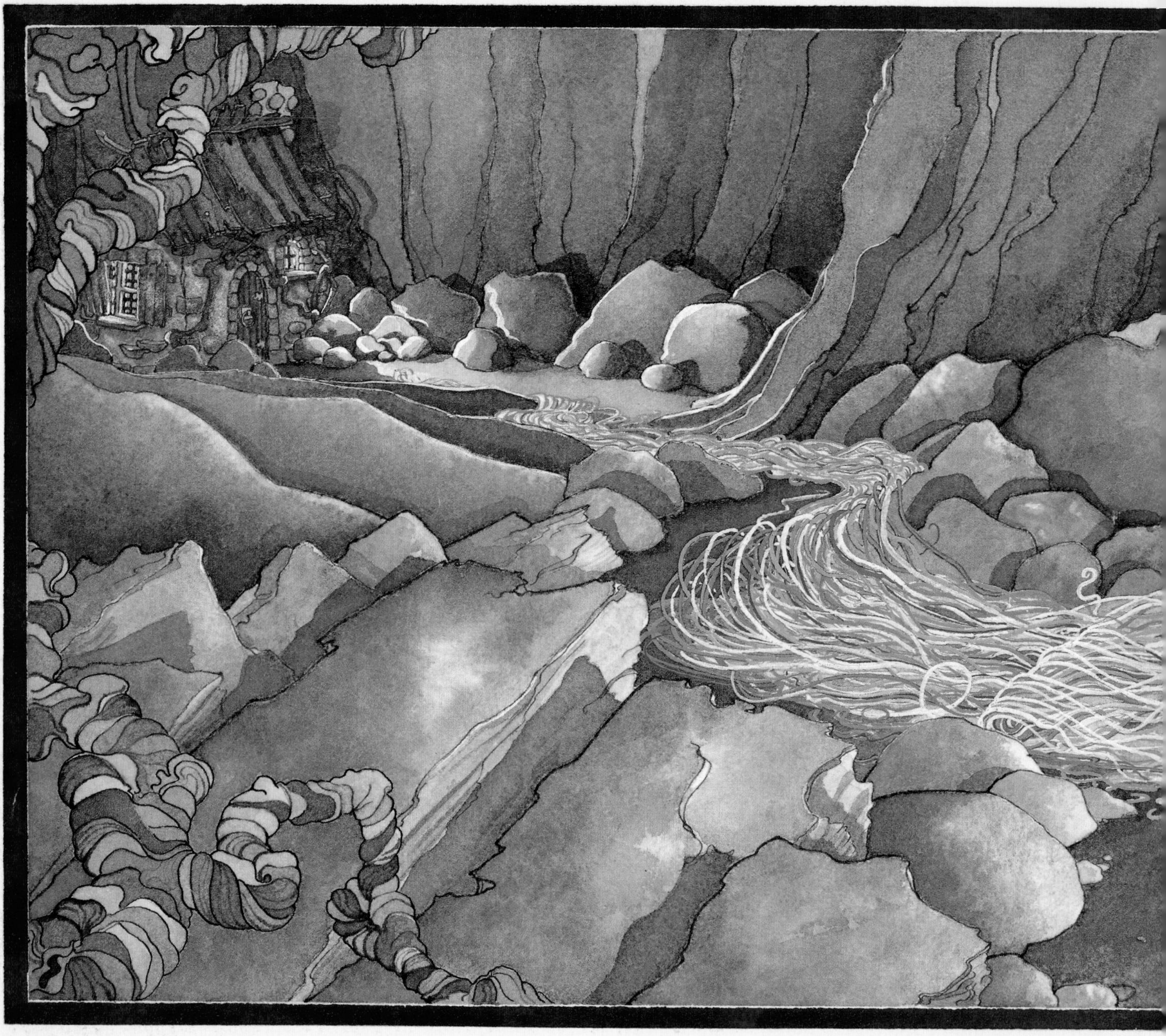

When Raina opened her eyes, she saw a small stone house in the distance. Then she heard crunching. Walking toward her was a little old man with a long white beard. He poked his cane at her and said, "I am Old Rinkrank. You have fallen

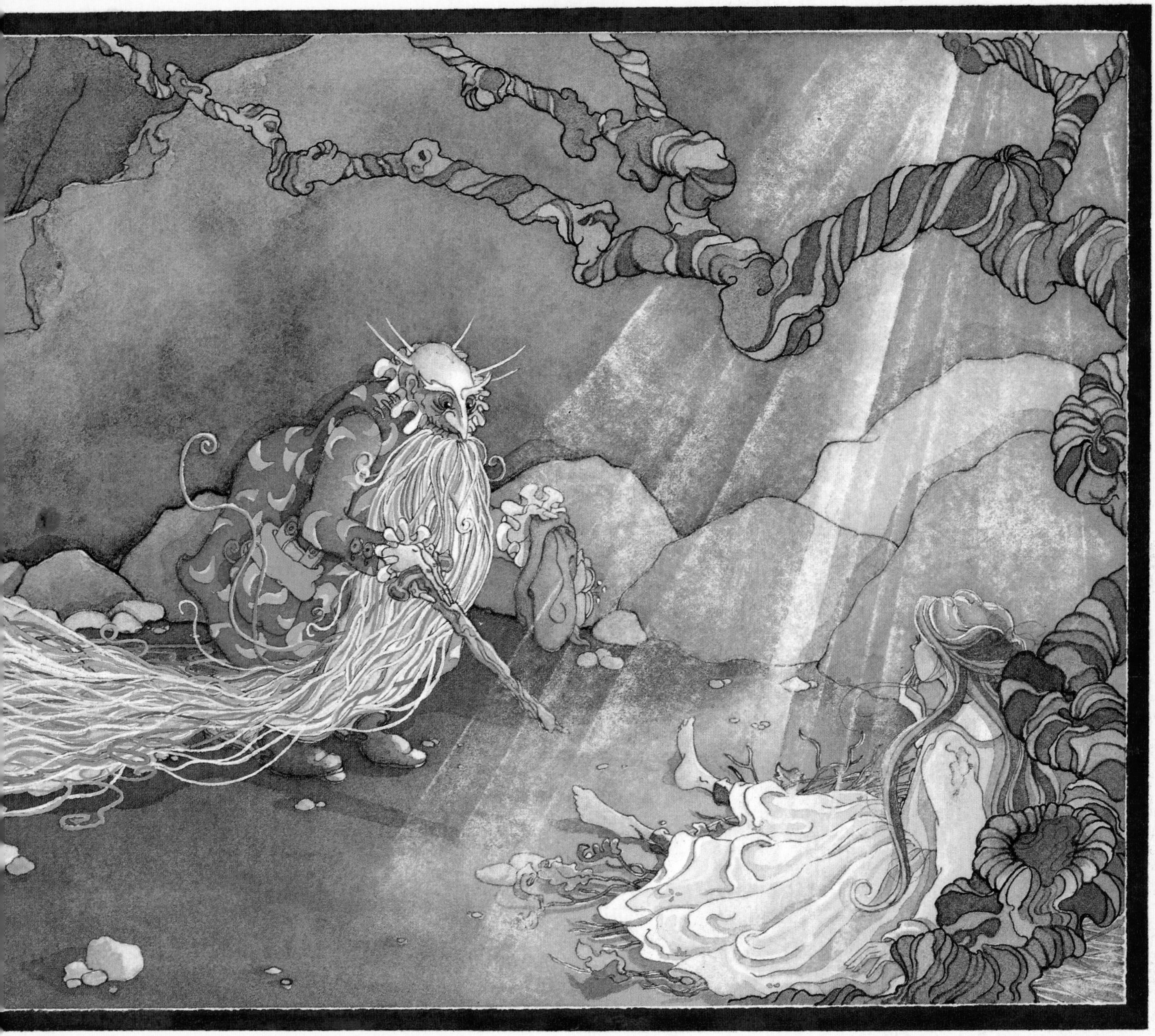

through a crack in the mountain, into my cave. You will never see the world again. If you wish to live, you must be my servant and do everything I say." And whether she wanted to or not, the princess had to obey.

Every day she had to stoke the fire and make his breakfast. Every day she had to clean the house and prepare the dinner. And every morning after breakfast, Old Rinkrank left the house, unlocked the shed, took a ladder, and climbed out of the cave. Every evening he came down the ladder with his pockets filled with gold and silver, which he buried in the earth.

As time passed, the princess forgot about her father. She forgot about the young man. With no one to speak to, she even forgot her own name. Every day she stoked the fire. She made the breakfast. She cleaned the house. She prepared the dinner.

Then one morning, after breakfast, Old Rinkrank suddenly said to her, "Enough time has passed. Now you must call me Old Rinkrank, and I will call you Mother Houserot."

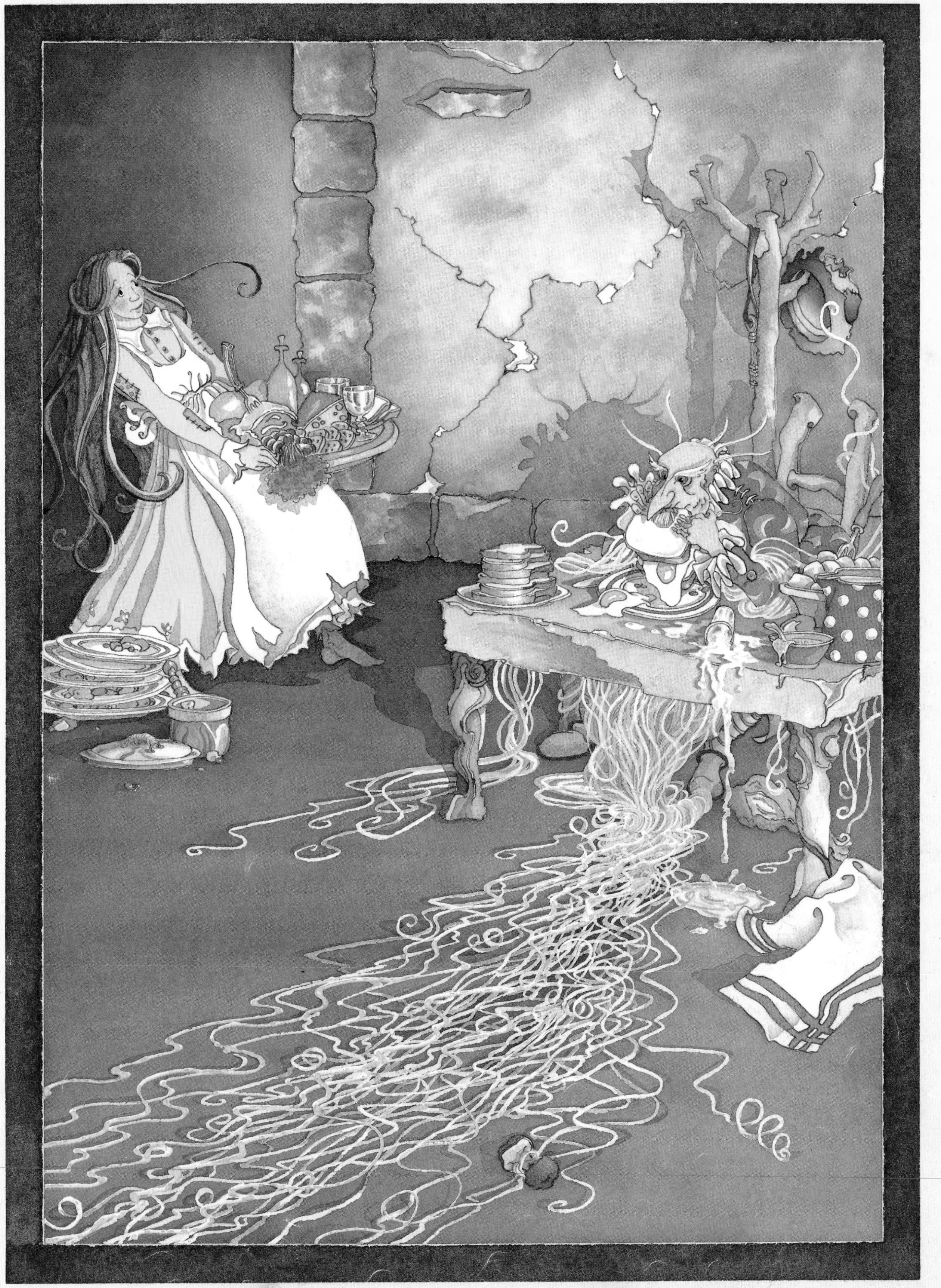

She watched him go, but she did not move. She repeated the name he had spoken: "Mother Houserot." *Rot?* she said to herself. Am I a rotting house? Who am I? What *is* my name?

Trying to remember her name, she looked about the house. In one of the cupboards she found her rose-colored cap. She held it in her hand and sat down. She knew she had to wash the dishes. She did not move. She sat there, and after a while she heard the sound of whistling. It was a merry whistling, and she realized she was remembering the young man whistling, *her* young man. A ray of sunshine, he had called her—and then she remembered her name.

At that moment, she knew what she would do. She put on her rose-colored cap. She did not wash the dishes. She did not clean the house. She did not prepare the dinner. She locked the front and back doors, opened the back window, and set a burning candle behind it. Then she sat down and waited.

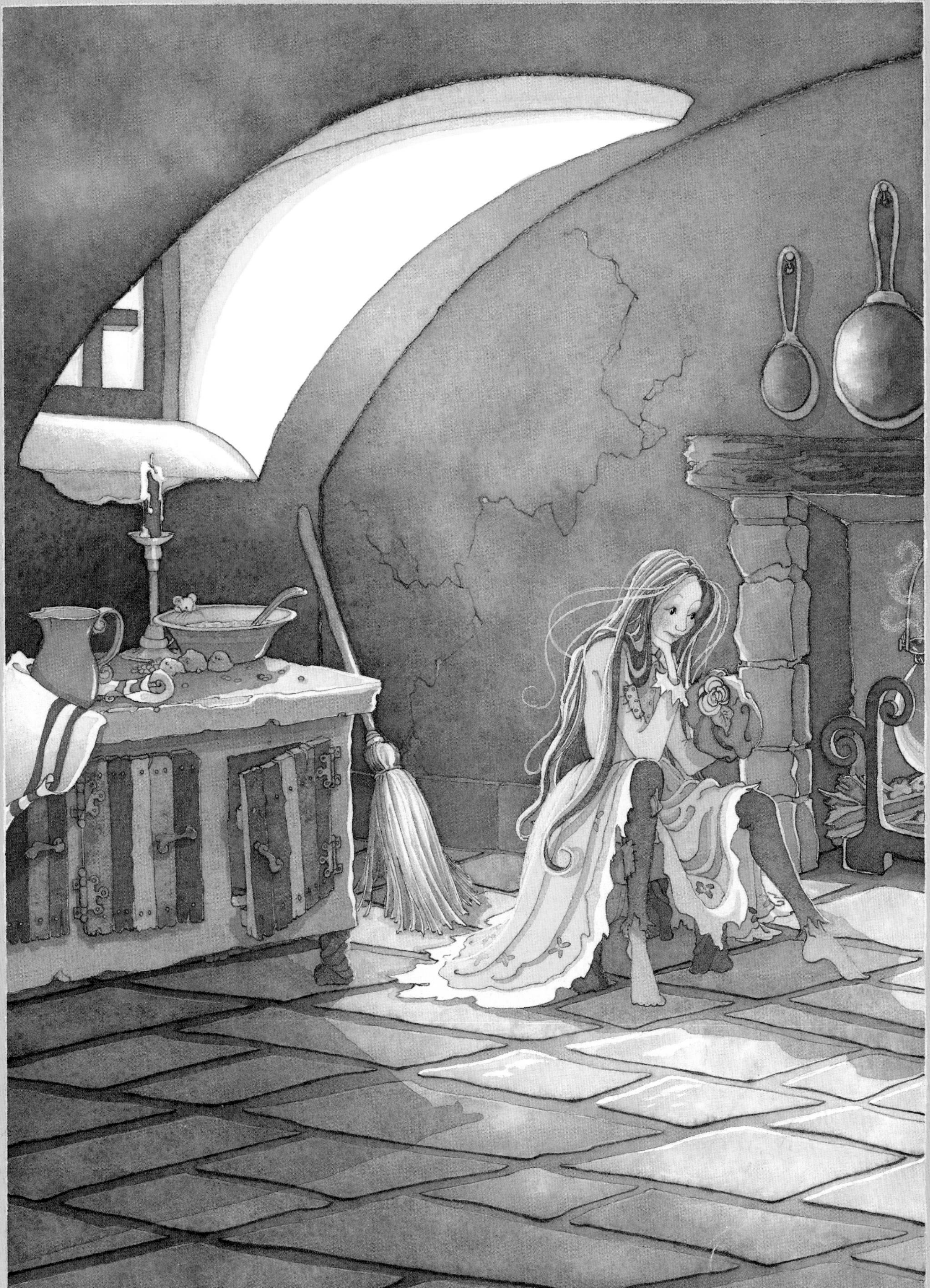

At dinnertime, Old Rinkrank came down the ladder. He buried his gold and silver and tried to enter the house. The door was locked. He knocked on the door and called out:

"Here I stand, Old Rinkrank,
on my weary worn-out foot.
Open the door, Mother Houserot."

She said: "I will not."
He knocked louder and cried:

"Here I stand, Old Rinkrank,
on my weary worn-out foot.
Open the door, Mother Houserot!"

She sat where she was, and she said: "I will not."
So he ran around to the back door and tried to pull it open. But it too was locked. He knocked on the door even louder and shouted:

"HERE I STAND, OLD RINKRANK,
ON MY WEARY WORN-OUT FOOT.
OPEN THIS DOOR, MOTHER HOUSEROT!"

And she said: "I will not."

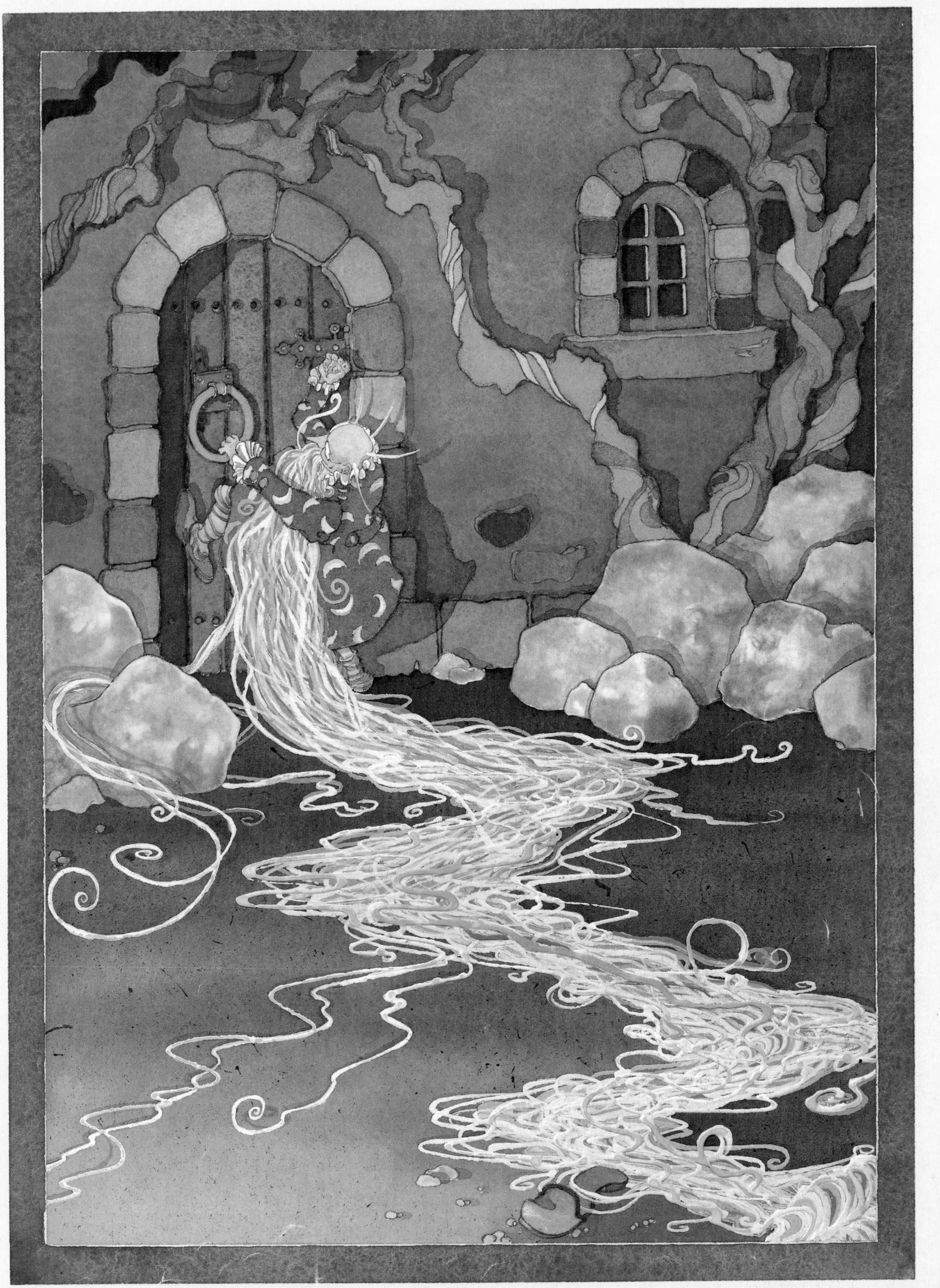

Old Rinkrank looked up and saw that a window was open. He wondered what she was doing inside the house. "I will take a peek," he said to himself. He stood on his tiptoes to look in, but as he did, she brought the window down on his beard.

"*Ohhhhhhhhohhhhhh*OHHHHH*ohhhh*OHHH*ohhhh!*" he wailed piteously. "Let me go!"

"No," she said.

"OHHHHHHH," he continued to wail. "Let me go!"

"Not until you give me the key in your pocket."

And whether he wanted to or not, Old Rinkrank had to give her his key.

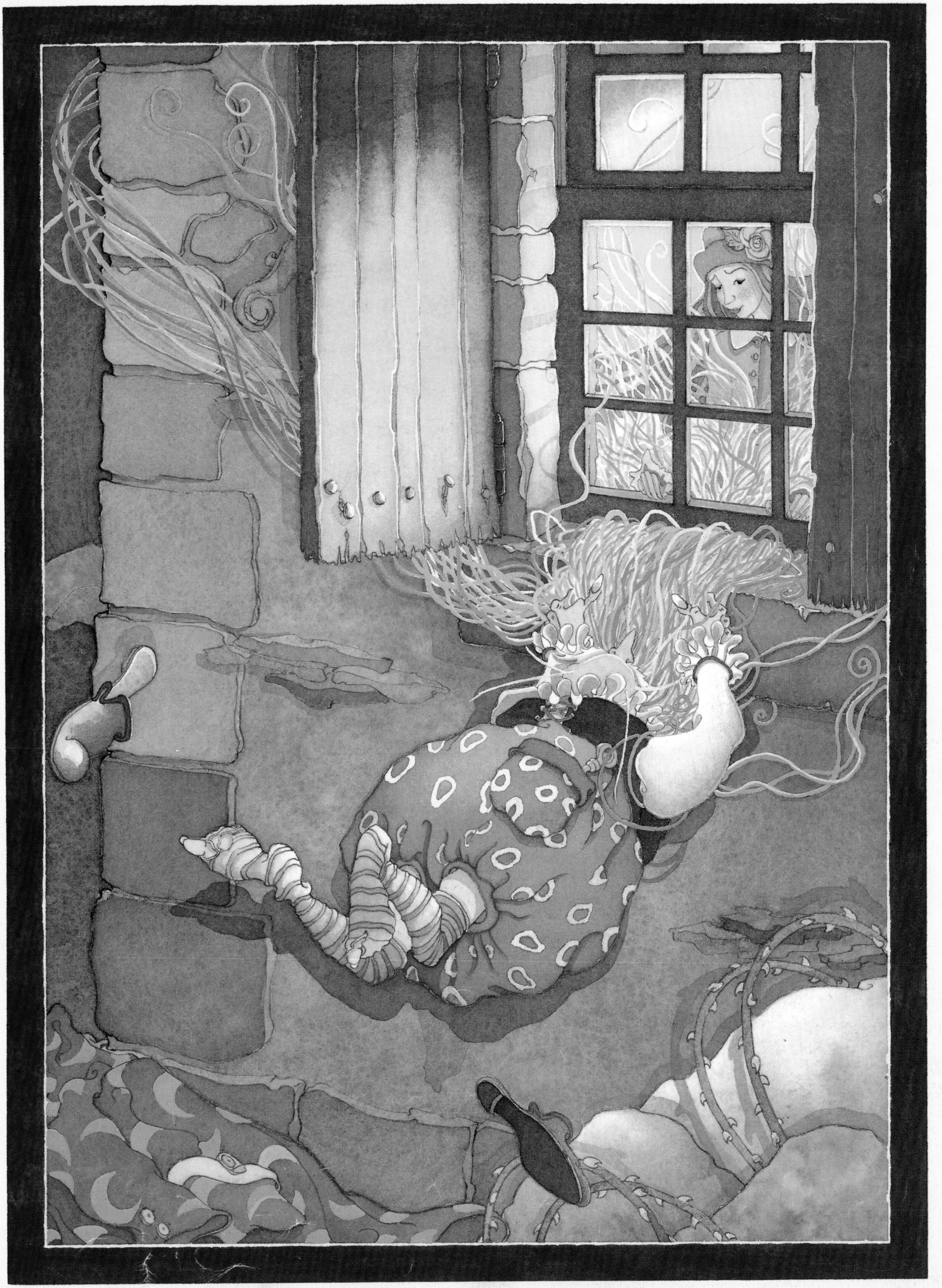

She unlocked the shed and took out the ladder. She tied a long orange ribbon to the window. She climbed the ladder, and when she was at the top, she pulled the ribbon, releasing Old Rinkrank. Then she looked up and gasped. She hadn't remembered how blue the sky was. As she walked home, she paused now and then to marvel at the sunlight on the stones and on the lime green trees.

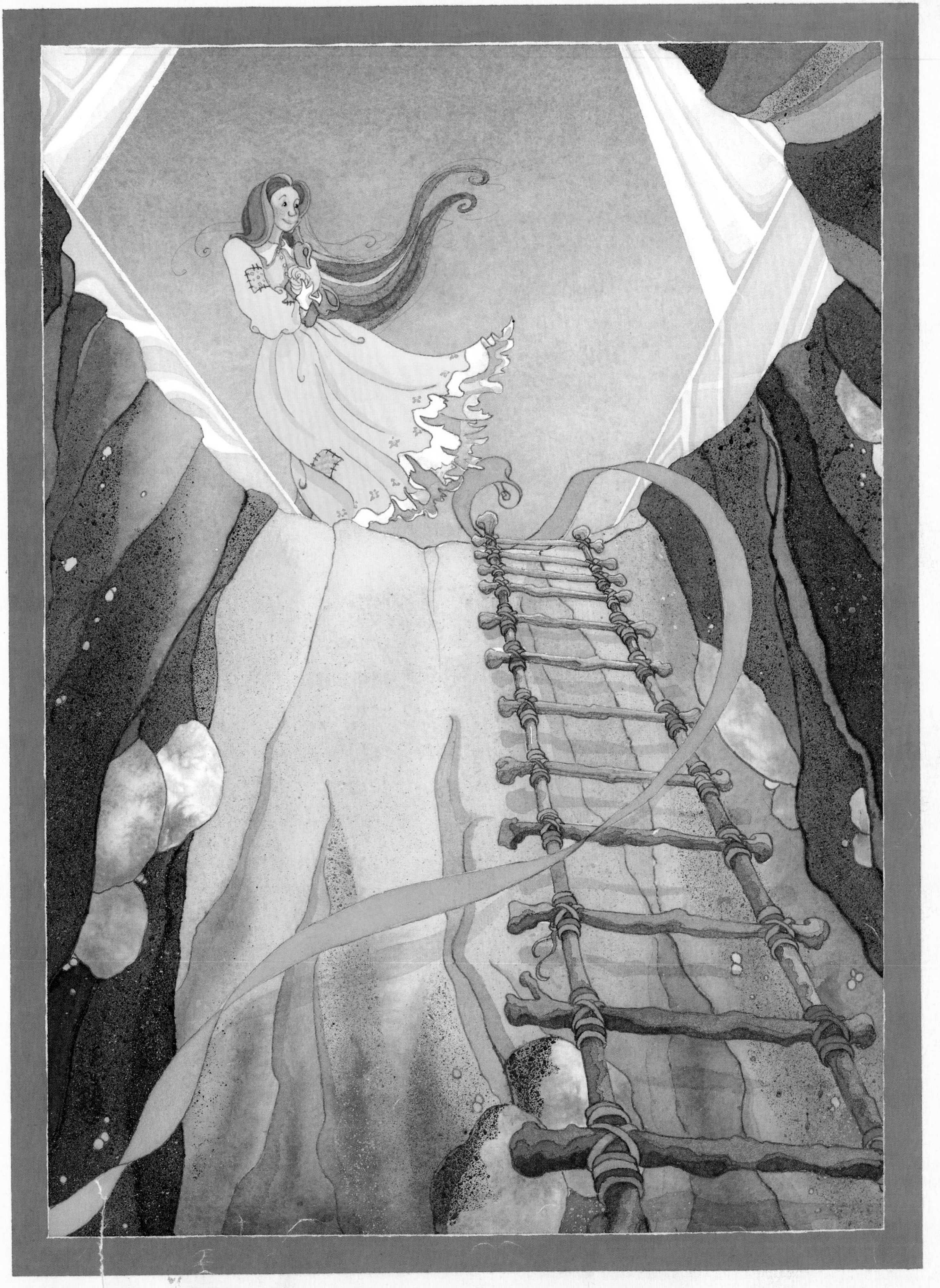

She did not go in the front gate of the palace but instead climbed over the back gate into the garden. There, sitting on a bench, was her father, with a young man. Raina hid behind a pear tree and whistled the song of the lark. The young man echoed her song. Raina whistled the song of the warbler. The young man stood up, puzzled, and walked toward the pear tree. He looked behind it, and there she was!

"The sunshine has returned!" Jared cried.

"Raina! Raina!" the king called. Rushing into her father's arms, Raina cried, "Father, I am home." The gardener shouted, "The princess has returned!" And from all over the palace the servants came to welcome Raina home.

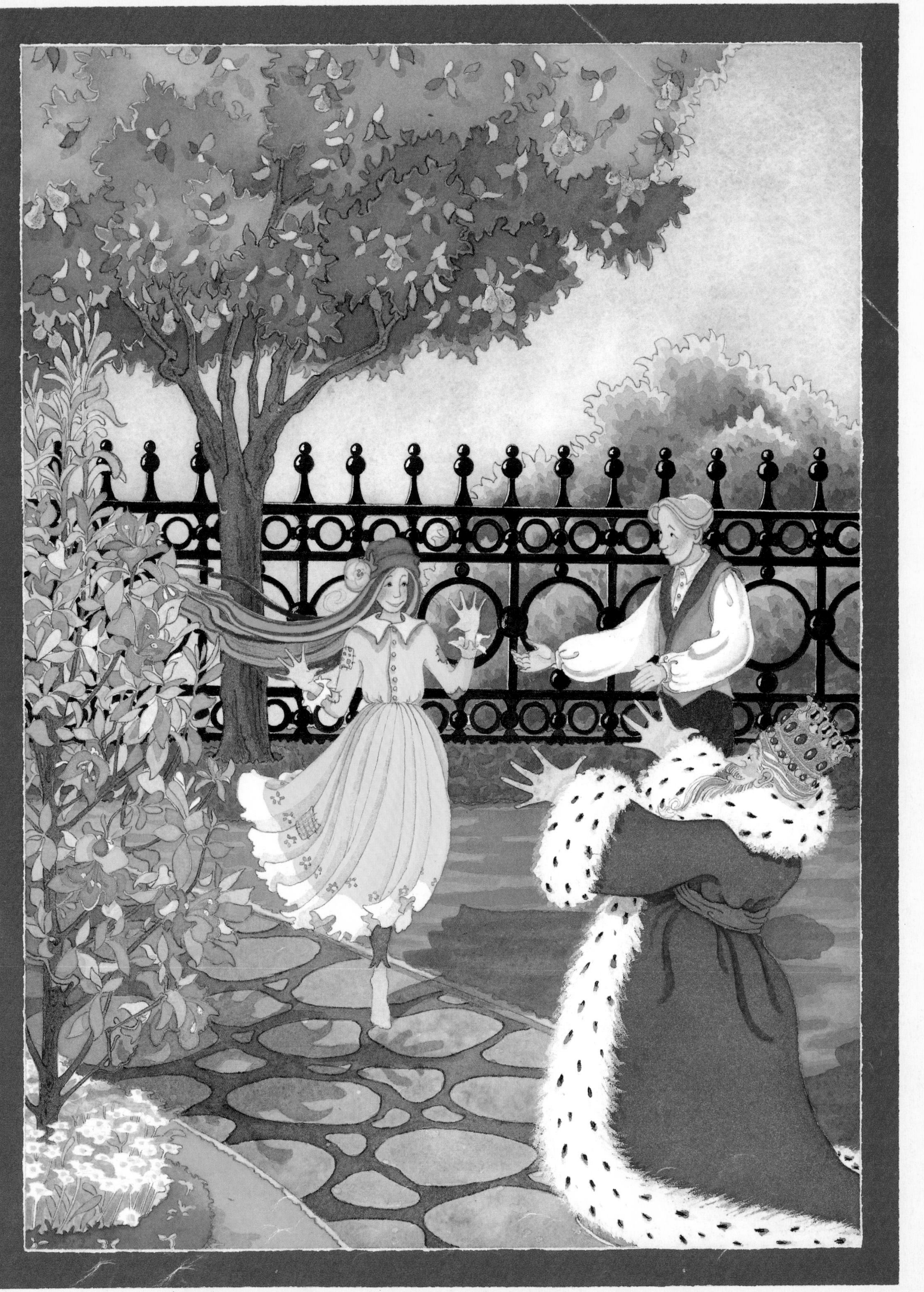

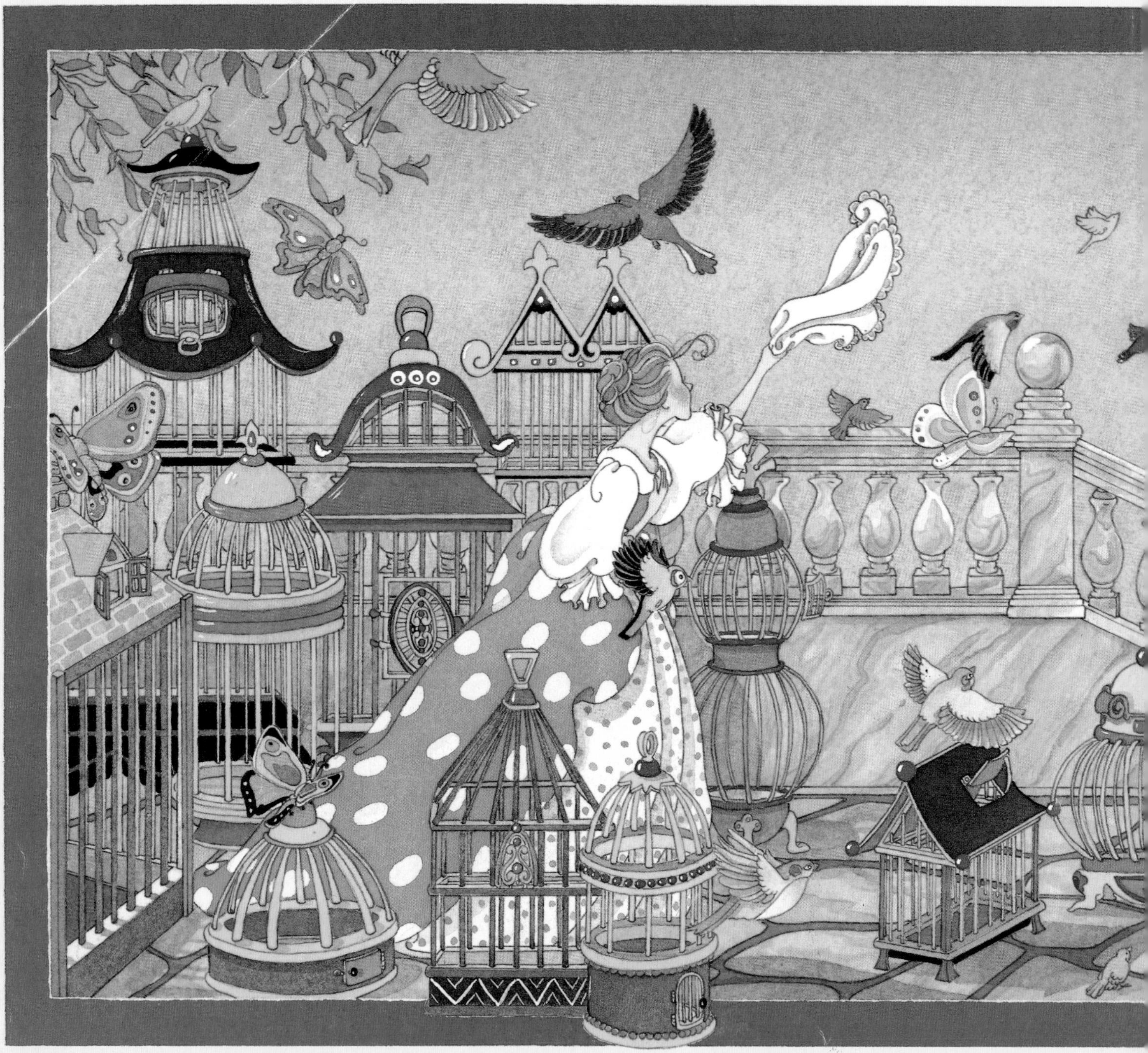

Raina greeted them and then went into the palace to see her birds. When she came to the first birdcage, she stopped. The bird did not sing. It was quiet. Raina too was still.

The next day Raina and Jared went through every

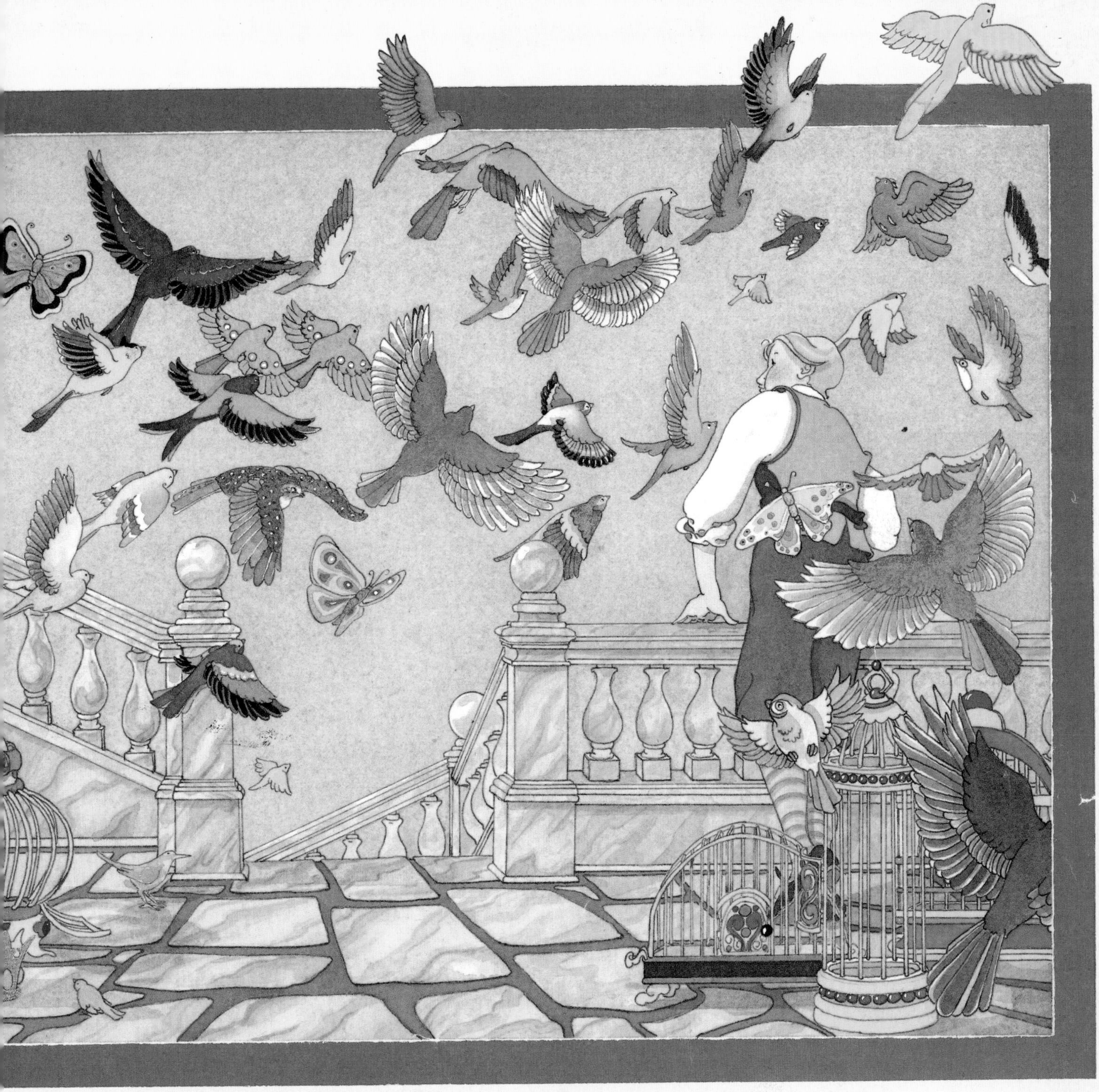

room in the palace and carried the birdcages outside.

Then, one by one, Raina opened each cage and whispered to each bird, "Fly home—fly free! Fly home! Fly free!"

Some time later, Raina said to her father, "I am going back to the cave."

"No!" her father protested.

"Yes," she said.

And Jared said, "I will go with her and help her."

Raina and Jared set out toward the glass mountain. They found the orange ribbon and slowly climbed down the ladder—

down,

down,

down,

to the bottom of the cave. They listened. There was no sound of crunching. Old Rinkrank had disappeared, but with his shovel they took turns digging up the gold and silver.

As Raina was digging, Jared held out a handful of the treasure and asked, "What will you do with all this gold and silver?"

Raina paused and then she answered, "I would like to make a beautiful garden filled with fruit trees and flowing streams where all living creatures can come and go."

"If you wish," Jared said, "we can build it together."

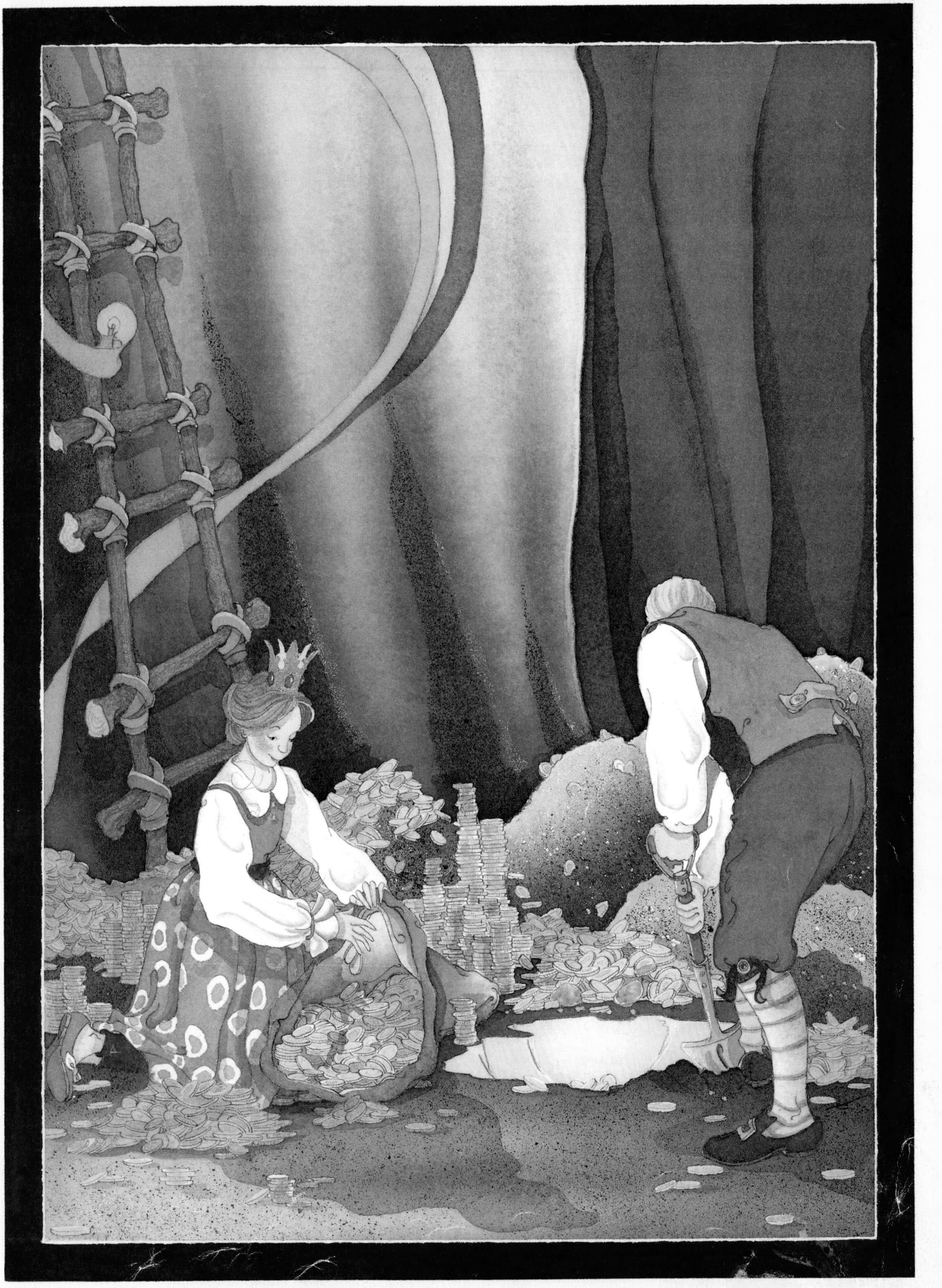

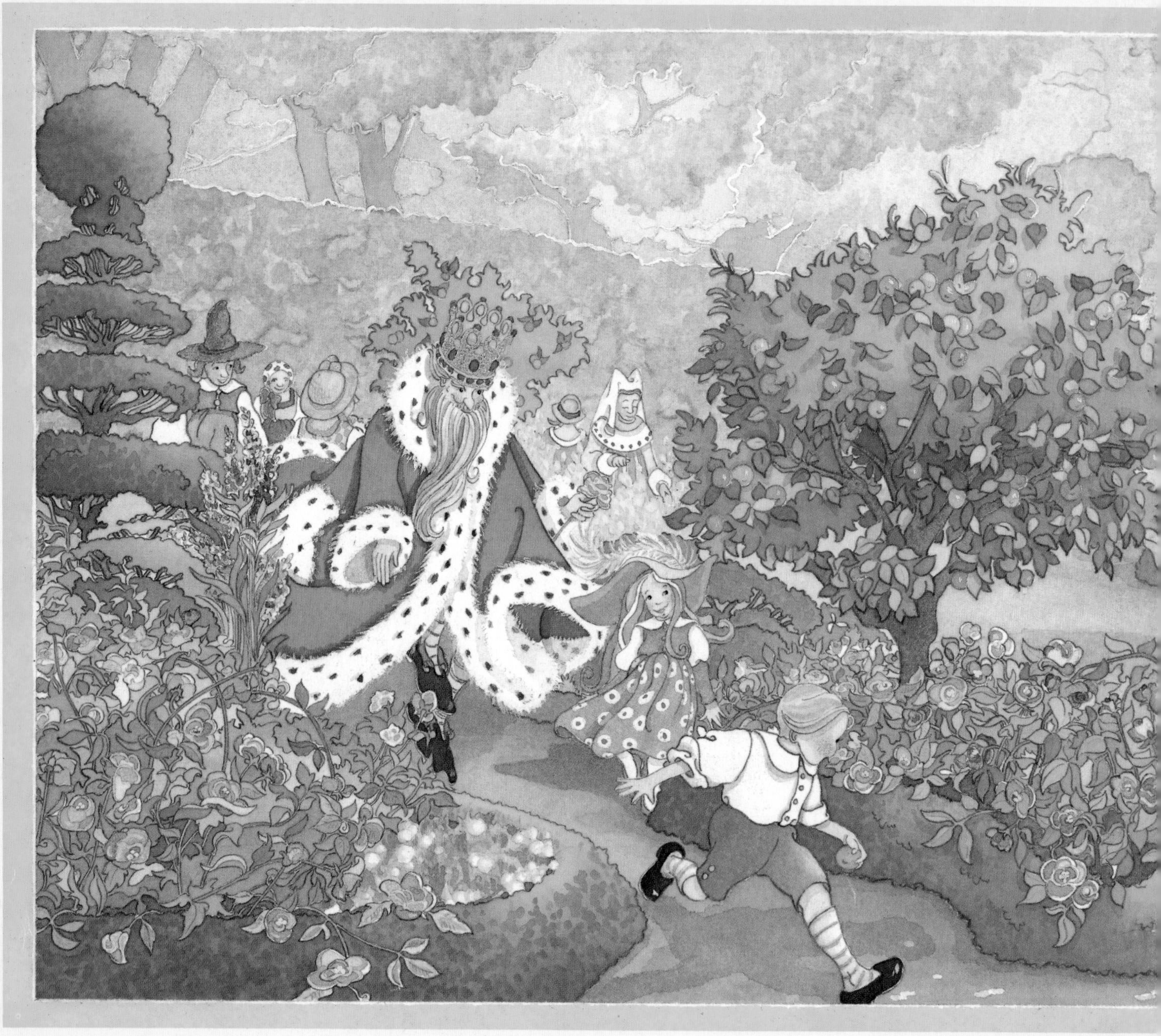

And that is what they did. When it was finished, they held their wedding in the garden they had created. Everyone in the town, young and old, was invited. The wedding celebration went on for seven

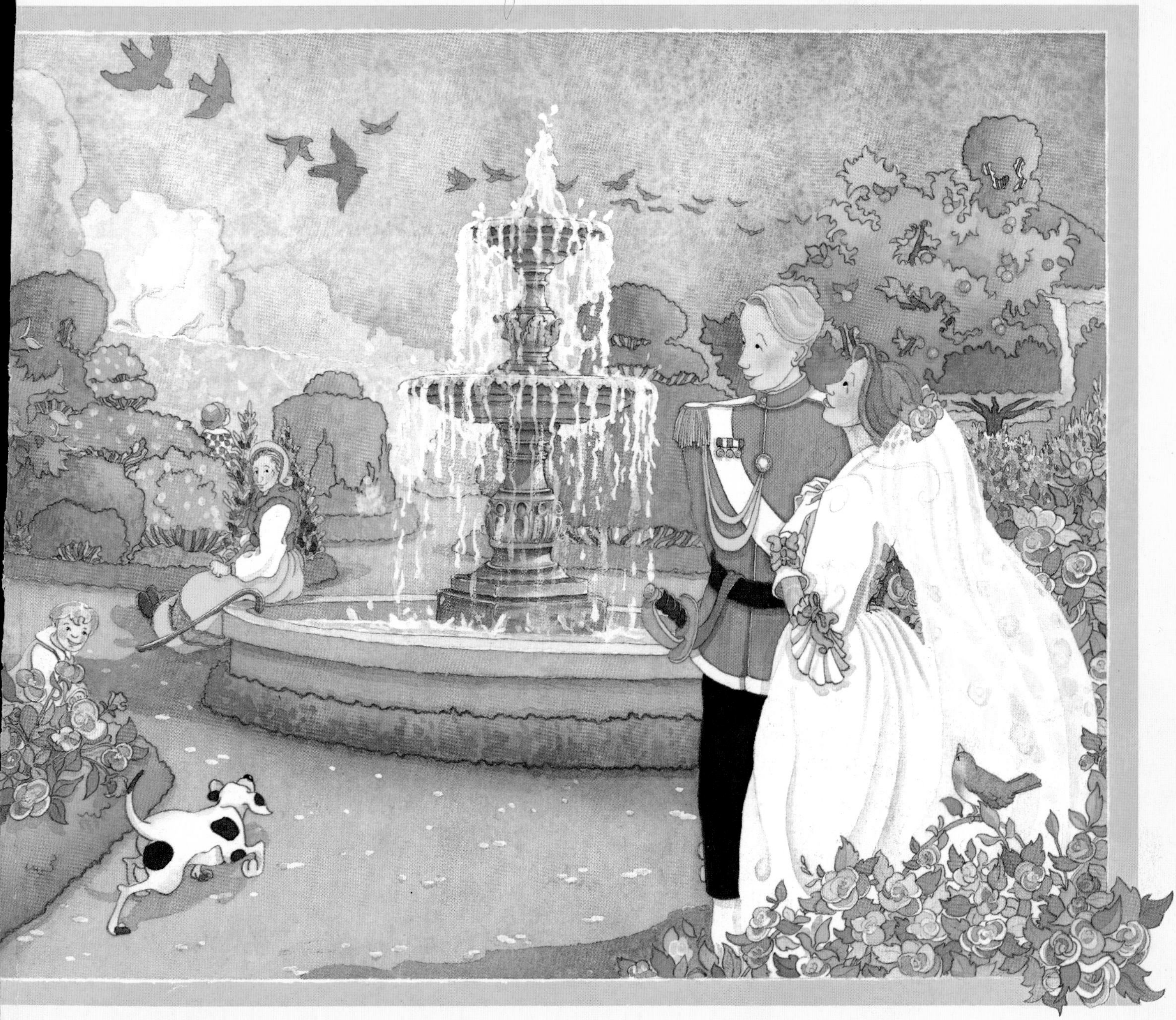

days and seven nights. On the last day, Raina toasted her bridegroom by whistling the song of the lark. Jared whistled a reply. And in the distance, a flock of larks echoed their song.

For Rachel Cloudstone Zucker and Joshua Goren,
newlyweds,

and Thich Nhat Hanh

AUTHOR'S NOTE

This story is adapted from the Grimm Brothers' story "Old Rinkrank," or "The Glass Mountain."
Twenty years ago, my friend Frank Roosevelt protested that the ending of "luxury and joy" was not suitable for
our times and needs. The Buddhist teacher Thich Nhat Hanh and the community of Plum Village inspired a
transformation in the story, so here, Frank, is your new ending.
My thanks to the many children and adults of Syracuse, New York; Columbus and Bloomington, Indiana;
and Rifle Creek, Beard, and Boulder, Colorado, who cheered on the emergence of Raina and Jared.
My special thanks to my editor Andrea Curley—the best of midwives.

Watercolors and gouache were used for the full-color illustrations.
The text type is 18-point Elysium Book.

Text copyright © 1999 by Diane Wolkstein
Illustrations copyright © 1999 by Louisa Bauer

Published by Morrow Junior Books
a division of William Morrow and Company, Inc.
1350 Avenue of the Americas, New York, NY 10019
www.williammorrow.com

Printed in Hong Kong by South China Printing Company (1988) Ltd.

10 9 8 7 6 5 4 3 2 1

Library of Congress Cataloging-in-Publication Data
Wolkstein, Diane.
The glass mountain / Diane Wolkstein; illustrated by Louisa Bauer.
p. cm.
"Adapted from the Grimm Brothers' story Old Rinkrank, also known as The glass mountain."
Summary: A king builds a glass mountain which any man who wants to marry his daughter must
climb, but when Princess Raina tries to help one suitor climb it, she falls through a deep crack and
is trapped in a deep cave.
ISBN 0-688-14847-6 (trade)––ISBN 0-688-14848-4 (library)
[1. Fairy tales.   2. Folklore—Germany.]   I. Bauer, Louisa, ill.   II. Title.   PZ8.W816G1 1999
398.2'0943'02—dc21   [E] 98-24036 CIP AC

DATE			